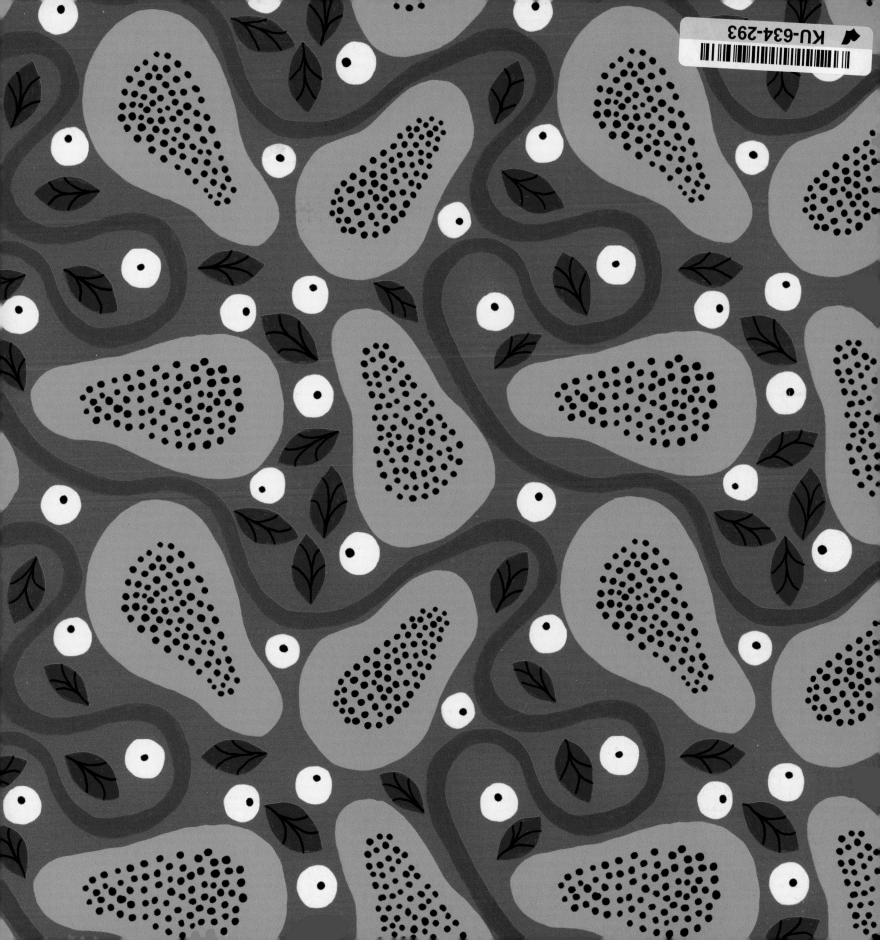

For Charlie xx – L.R.
To Eddie and Bungle, my wild animals – M.F.

First published 2022 by Macmillan Children's Books
an imprint of Pan Macmillan
The Smithson, 6 Briset Street, London EC1M 5NR
EU representative: Macmillan Publishers Ireland Limited
1st Floor, The Liffey Trust Centre, 117–126 Sheriff Street Upper, Dublin 1, D01 YC43
Associated companies throughout the world

www.panmacmillan.com

ISBN: 978-1-5290-7509-0

Text copyright © Lucy Rowland 2022
Illustrations copyright © Monika Forsberg 2022

1 3 5 7 9 8 6 4 2

A CIP catalogue record for this book is available
from the British Library.

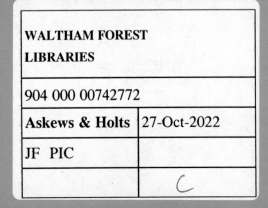

This book belongs to

....

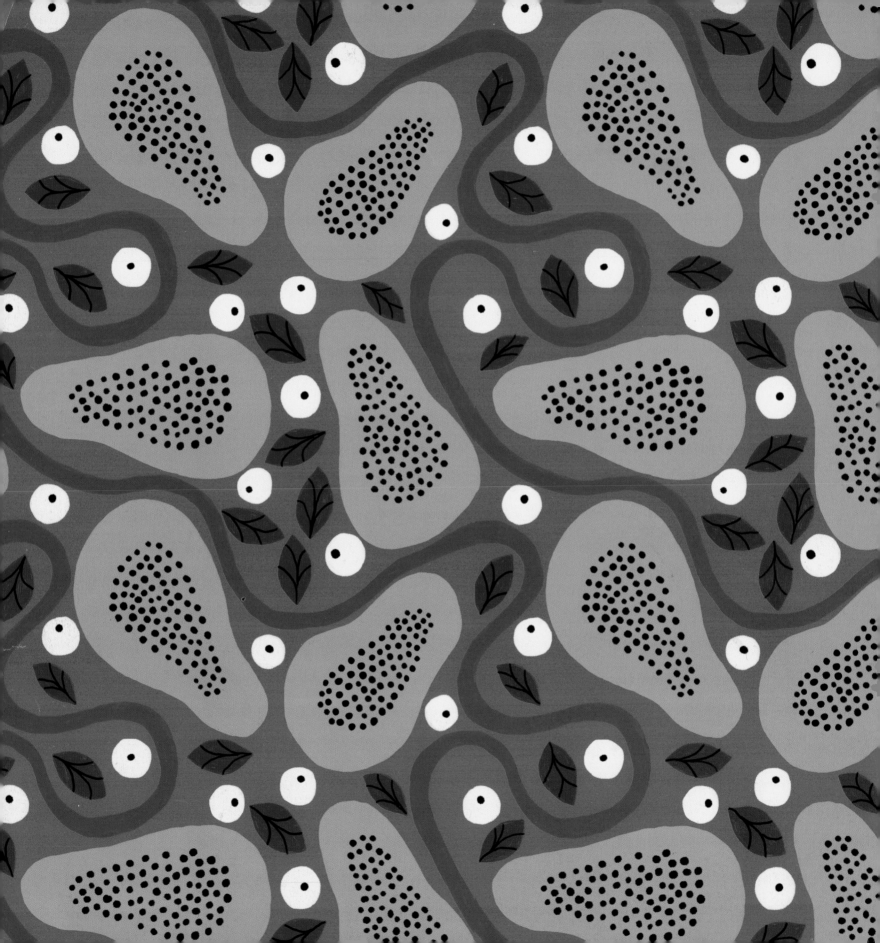

Night Night Sleep Tight

Jungle Animals

LUCY ROWLAND

MONIKA FORSBERG

Macmillan Children's Books

Jungle leaves sway overhead,
Let's put the animals to bed.

Tiger cubs are
curled up tight.
Time for them
to say goodnight.

Night night tigers –
no more roaring.
Settle down, you'll
soon be snoring.

Now look up into the trees . . .

Night night monkeys,
no more play.

Rest until
another day.

In the river...
crocodiles!

Night night crocs,
you've cleaned your teeth.
Your blanket's here to snooze beneath.

Night night
elephants
so calm,

Snuggled underneath the palm.

Baby parrot,
stop that talking!

Night night elephants,

Night night parrot.

Bye bye jungle. Now we're done.
Night night, sleep tight, everyone.

Night night tigers,

Night night monkeys,

Night night crocodiles,

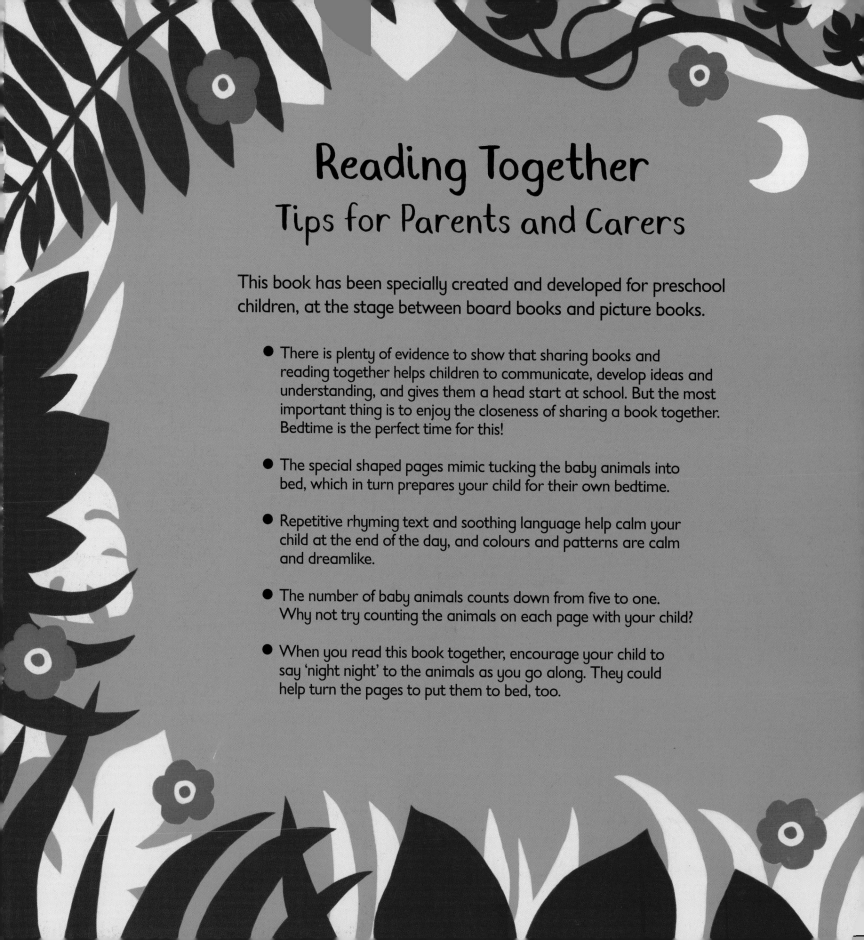

Reading Together
Tips for Parents and Carers

This book has been specially created and developed for preschool children, at the stage between board books and picture books.

- There is plenty of evidence to show that sharing books and reading together helps children to communicate, develop ideas and understanding, and gives them a head start at school. But the most important thing is to enjoy the closeness of sharing a book together. Bedtime is the perfect time for this!

- The special shaped pages mimic tucking the baby animals into bed, which in turn prepares your child for their own bedtime.

- Repetitive rhyming text and soothing language help calm your child at the end of the day, and colours and patterns are calm and dreamlike.

- The number of baby animals counts down from five to one. Why not try counting the animals on each page with your child?

- When you read this book together, encourage your child to say 'night night' to the animals as you go along. They could help turn the pages to put them to bed, too.

Night Night, Sleep Tight!

A good night's sleep can help support your child's growth and development. Here are some top tips to help create a calm, peaceful bedtime, from the experts at The Sleep Charity.

- A regular routine can help your child's mind and body prepare for sleep. Start the routine about an hour before their bedtime.

- During the routine it helps to dim the lights and draw the curtains — darkness will encourage your child's body to create the sleep hormone, melatonin.

- Switch off screens in the hour before bedtime and choose relaxing activities such as having a bath, doing a jigsaw, or colouring a picture.

- Help your child understand that bedtime is approaching by letting them tuck their toys into bed and say goodnight to each one.

- Use the same calming piece of music each evening to set the scene for a relaxing routine.

- A story is the perfect way to end the day. Let your child choose which story they want to read, so they feel they have some control.

- Using the same book can help too — young children love repetition and routine. Snuggle up with them, get comfy, and read softly and slowly.

- End the day with hugs and kisses before leaving them to get a good night's sleep.

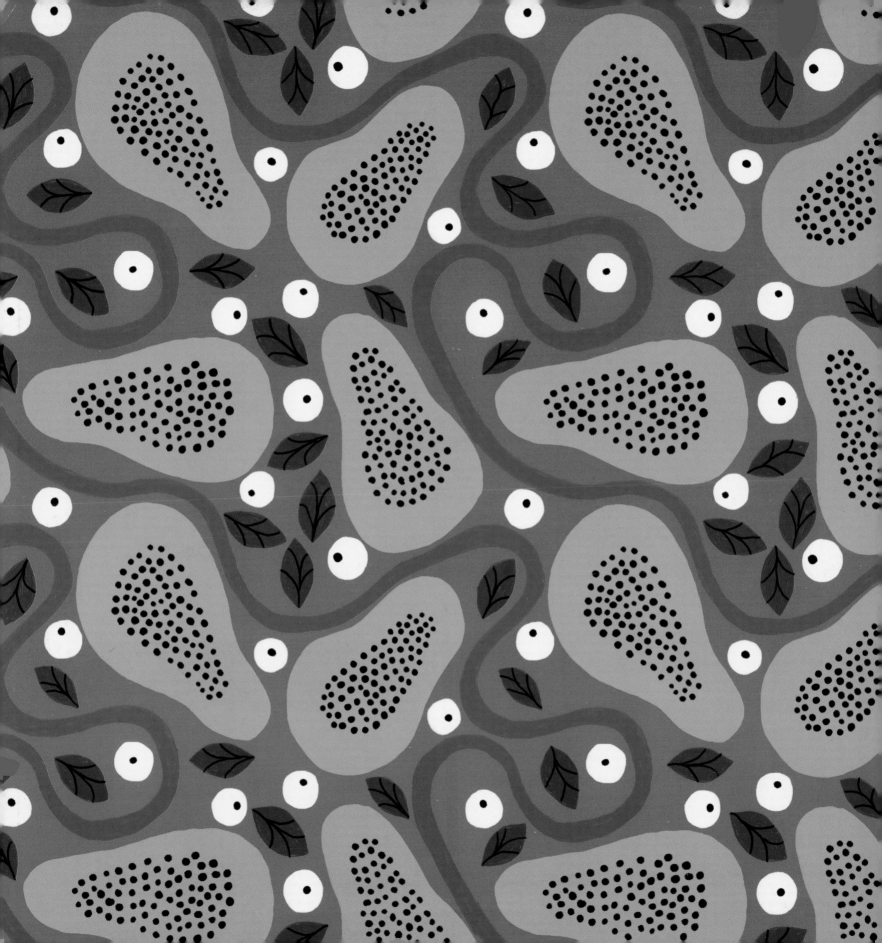

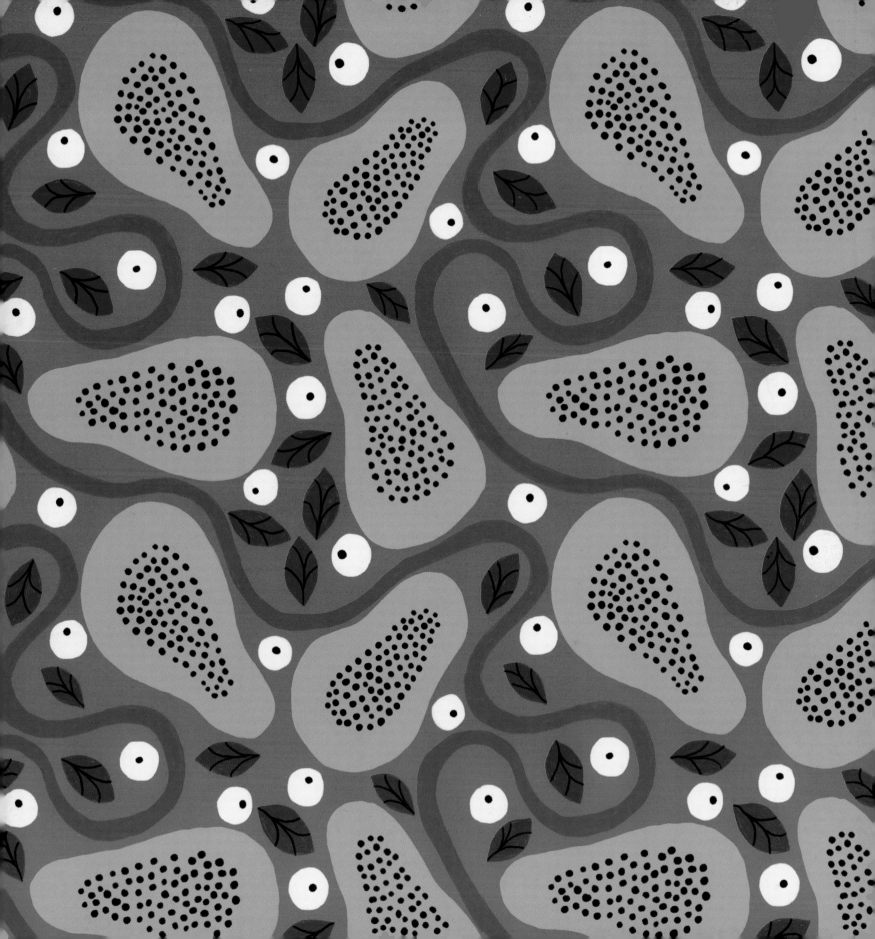